Copyright © 1991 by Shirley Hughes
First published in Great Britain by Walker Books Ltd. All rights reserved.
No part of this book may be reproduced or utilized in any form or by any means,
electronic or mechanical, including photocopying, recording or by any
information storage and retrieval system, without permission in writing from the
Publisher. Inquiries should be addressed to Lothrop, Lee & Shepard Books,
a division of William Morrow & Company, Inc., 105 Madison Avenue, New York,
New York 10016. Printed in Hong Kong.

First U.S. edition   1   2   3   4   5   6   7   8   9   10

Library of Congress Cataloging in Publication Data
Hughes, Shirley. Wheels: a tale of Trotter Street / Shirley Hughes.
p.   cm.   Summary: Carlos is jealous of his friend Billy's new bicycle and
desperately wants a new one of his own for his upcoming birthday.
ISBN 0-688-09880-0. — ISBN 0-688-09881-9 (lib. bdg.)   [1. Bicycles and bicycling—
Fiction.   2. Friendship—Fiction.   3. Birthdays—Fiction.]   I. Title.
II. Title: Wheels.   PZ7.H87395Tal   1991   [E]—dc20
90-40473 CIP AC

A Tale of Trotter Street

Wheels

Shirley Hughes

Lothrop, Lee & Shepard Books

New York

Spring at last! The Easter holidays had arrived and the wheels were out on Trotter Street. Sanjit Lal zipped along on his roller skates, wearing a smart crash helmet. Little Pete Patterson rode his red tricycle, ring-a-ding-dinging the bell to let everyone know he was coming.

Harvey and Barney took turns on Barney's skateboard, and Mae pushed her baby sister Holly in a brand new buggy. Some of the big girls and boys had wonderful, new, full-size bikes, even racers! They gathered at the corner to show them off. Carlos and Billy had their old bikes.

Billy's mum looked after Carlos in the school holidays, while *his* mum was at work. When she took Billy's baby brother to the park in the afternoon, Carlos and Billy came too and brought their bikes. They were not old enough to ride on the road, of course. It was too dangerous.

The park was the best place to ride. There was a smooth, wide path that went round the play area, then into a steep slope. You could whizz down it, cornering at high speed, and freewheel the rest of the way, past the old bandstand until, braking gently, you ended up at the bottom by the lake where the ducks swam.

The little kids playing and the mums chatting on the benches and the old lady who came to feed the birds all stopped what they were doing and stared as Carlos and Billy flew past. Whooosh!

There was a narrow, humpbacked bridge over the lake. Carlos
and Billy thought it was exciting to race their bikes up one side
and down the other. Sometimes Carlos won and sometimes Billy.
But if Mr. Low, the park keeper, saw them, he soon put a stop to it.
He was very strict about people behaving well in his park. Mr. Low
did not seem to like fast riding at all, not even on the paths.

Orville, his assistant, was not quite so strict. Sometimes, when
Mr. Low went off to have a cup of tea in his hut, Orville would call
out encouraging things to Carlos and Billy as they raced by.

All the same, Carlos and Billy both wished they had better bikes.

"You can get up a lot more speed on a big bike," said Billy. "They have gears too."

"I've seen one I like in a shop," said Carlos. "Blue and silver with a pump to match."

"I'm going to ask for a new bike for my birthday," said Billy. "It's very soon now."

"It's my birthday soon as well," said Carlos, "and I'm going to get a new bike too."

Carlos asked his mum about this. He had asked her before and he asked her again that evening. But his mum said that new bikes were very expensive. She explained that it was difficult for her to save up for things like bikes. She worked in a bakery and often brought home nice fruit cake and cream buns for Carlos and his big brother, Marco—but not very much money.

"Marco's got a proper bike," moaned Carlos.

"He's older than you," said Mum, "and he needs it for his Saturday job. He's saving up for a new mountain bike. When you're bigger, you can learn to ride his old one."

"But I need a new bike *now*," Carlos said.

Mum only answered, "We'll have to see . . . ."

On the afternoon of his birthday, Billy proudly brought his brand-new bike to the park. It was orange, with shiny silver handlebars. Everyone gathered round to admire it. Even Orville left his work to come and have a look.

"Race you!" Billy called out to Carlos as he pulled away and glided off down the path.

It was not much of a race. Billy won easily. Carlos felt silly pedaling furiously behind, crouched over the handlebars of his old bike. His legs felt too long and his knees kept getting in the way.

After a while Billy's mum suggested that Billy should give Carlos a turn on his new bike, which he very kindly did.

But when Carlos had swooped down the hill like a bird once or twice, he had to give the beautiful bike back to Billy.

In the end, Carlos gave up wanting to race. There was no point.
He threw down his old bike by the lake and sat by himself, tossing
pebbles into the water.

He felt cross with Billy. He even felt cross with the ducks who came swimming over to see if he had any bread.

"You wait! You wait till it's my birthday!" he told them.

On the evening before his birthday, Carlos kept wondering if Mum had managed to get him a bike. He thought she could have hidden one in the shed behind their block of flats.

He even secretly slipped out and tried the shed door, but it was locked. Was there a bike inside? He looked through a crack, but he couldn't see anything.

Mum had promised that tomorrow she would bring home a very special cake from the shop—a birthday cake for Carlos! She said that he could ask Billy round for tea. But Carlos didn't want Billy to come to his birthday tea.

In bed that night, Carlos was too excited to sleep.

He kept imagining getting a new bike: a big bike, a blue and silver bike, a bike that was even better and faster than Billy's, which he could show off in the park. He crept to the window and looked down at the shed. There was a light on in there! He could see it shining up through the skylight in the roof. He watched for a long time. Then he went back to bed.

In the morning Mum gave
Carlos a big birthday hug.
Marco had gone off early,
but he had left a card
on the kitchen table
with some bears in a
spaceship and "Happy
Birthday, Carlos" written
inside it. There were some

parcels on the table too, all wrapped in fancy paper.

"Aren't you going to open them?" asked Mum, beaming.

Carlos pulled off the papers one by one. There was a jigsaw
puzzle, a new jacket in dazzling red and green, just like the ones
the big boy bikers wore, and a toy car with remote control.
Carlos had wanted one ever since he had seen them in a shop,
and he was very pleased. But he knew at once that there was
no new bike.

"Marco's going to give you his present when he comes in at teatime," Mum told him.

Carlos knew that Marco's present could not possibly be a new bike. He would not have nearly enough money for that. Inside, Carlos could not help feeling bitterly disappointed.

When Mum asked him if he would like to go and play with Billy that morning and show him his new things, Carlos said no—he would rather go to the shop with Mum. So he took his new car and played with it in the back of the bakery while his mum served the customers. The car went very well. Everyone made a great fuss of Carlos when they heard it was his birthday. One lady bought him a chocolate cream cake and another gave him some money for his piggy bank.

When they got home, Mum opened a box and brought out a truly
wonderful cake. It was pink and white and covered in icing shells
and swirls, with silver holders for the candles. There was a plate
of fancy pastries too, and ice cream. Carlos ate a lot of everything.
But when the time came to light his candles, he missed having
Billy to help him blow them out.

Then Marco walked in. He got hold of Carlos and swung him round, singing "Happy Birthday to you!" Then he ate a very large slice of cake.

"Want to find out what I've got for you?" said Marco. "Follow me."

Carlos followed Marco downstairs. All the way down, Carlos was wondering what Marco was going to give him.

He knew it could not be a bike. So what was it? They walked right past the shed. Then at last Carlos saw his present!

It was a go-cart! A real go-cart! It had proper steering and rubber wheels and a seat, and it was painted bright red. Marco had made it himself. Carlos was too surprised to speak. Never, ever, in his

wildest dreams, had he imagined owning a go-cart! He looked at it for a long time. He stroked its wheels and its little seat. Then he put his head against Marco's arm. "Thanks, Marco," he said.

It was the last day of the holidays. Most of Trotter Street had
turned up in the park for the big event: the Non-Bicycle Race!
The starters were already lined up—Sanjit, Sam, and Ruby Roberts
were on roller skates; Harvey and Barney had skateboards.

Jim Zolinski and Brains Barrington were in their box-on-wheels,
Frankie had borrowed a scooter, and Mae and Debbie had one
roller skate each. Carlos was at the controls of his new go-cart,
with Billy crouching behind him. Now Josie lifted the starter's flag . . . .

Ready, steady, GO! Cheering mums, dads, and toddlers lined the track. The Bird Lady was there, and Orville too. Even Mr. Low popped his head round the door of his hut to watch, though mostly to keep an eye on his flowerbeds.

Past the play area, into the steep slope, gaining speed, then cornering wildly, sometimes crashing but managing to scramble on again, weaving, coasting, trundling they went—all the way down to the lake.

And who came first? Carlos and Billy in the wonderful go-cart, of course!